Nonna Tell Me a Story

LIDIA'S EGG-CITING FARM ADVENTURE

LIDIA BASTIANICH
Illustrated by Renée Graef

WITHDRAWN

RP | KIDS
PHILADELPHIA • LONDON

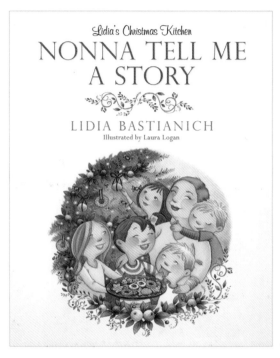

Lidia's Christmas Kitchen:
Nonna Tell Me a Story

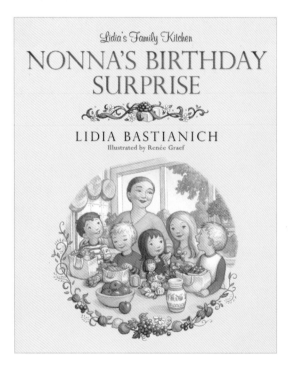

Lidia's Family Kitchen:
Nonna's Birthday Surprise

It is with much love and affection that I dedicate this book to my Nonna Rosa, my maternal grandmother. In honoring her, I also applaud all the farmers of the world that today supply us with food which has been grown with a consciousness to our well-being and in harmony with the ecological needs of the earth.

For me, it was in my Grandma Rosa's courtyard where I first played with chickens, fed them, cleaned their coops, and collected their eggs and understood the cycle of food. Nonna Rosa instilled in me respect for the land, the garden, and all the courtyard animals—goats, pigs, ducks, geese, rabbits, and donkeys—that lived as part of our small, rural community and helped to provide food for us. She gifted me with my everlasting childhood food memories by sharing the simplest things in life—seasonal food, a table full of family, and most of all, the love and understanding of it all.

Grazie,
Lidia

Books published by Running Press are available at special discounts for bulk purchases
in the United States by corporations, institutions, and other organizations. For more information,
please contact the Special Markets Department at the Perseus Books Group, 2300 Chestnut Street, Suite 200,
Philadelphia, PA 19103, or call (800) 810-4145, ext. 5000, or e-mail special.markets@perseusbooks.com.

ISBN 978-0-7624-5126-5
Library of Congress Control Number: 2013937585

9   8   7   6   5   4   3   2   1
Digit on the right indicates the number of this printing

Back cover photo: Diana DeLucia
Designed by Frances J. Soo Ping Chow
Illustrated by Renée Graef
Edited by Lisa Cheng
Typography: Perpetua, Murray Hill, and Univers

Published by Running Press Kids
An Imprint of Running Press Book Publishers
A Member of the Perseus Books Group
2300 Chestnut Street
Philadelphia, PA 19103-4371

Visit us on the web!
www.runningpress.com/rpkids
www.lidiasitaly.com

Dear Reader,

Many of us eat chicken or eggs every week, even every day. Sometimes we wonder: *Which came first, the chicken or the egg?* But how often do we *really* think about these important foods? Take the egg, so small and simple yet so miraculous. For many kids, eggs are pristine white things in cartons lining grocery-store refrigerators. And chicken? That's pink, squishy stuff wrapped in plastic or crispy little nuggets, sometimes shaped like dinosaurs!

As a child in my grandparents' courtyard in Istria, we raised our own chickens. I played with them, fed them, cleaned their coops, and collected their eggs. I was thankful when a chicken gave a fresh egg for my breakfast, or more importantly, its life to be turned into a good sauce for our Sunday pasta. Whether chicken, eggs, or other foods, I invite you to join the conversation—thinking more about what we eat, buy, and farm. Our choices today can help build healthy bodies, strong communities, and a cleaner planet for generations to come.

Andrij Bostich

It was a cool, starry night. Nonni Lidia and her grandchildren were gathered in her cozy living room having a sleepover and telling spooky stories. Olivia was just finishing an extra-scary one. . . .

"Then suddenly . . . ," she whispered. "Yellow eyes glowed. Sharp teeth flashed. And a spooky fox jumped out of the forest—*BOO!*"

"AHHHHH!" shrieked Julia, hugging her doll Lucia tightly.

"Don't be such a chicken!" teased Lorenzo, while Miles chuckled.

Nonni Lidia smiled at Julia. "You know," she said. "Chickens are pretty special."

"Chickens are pink and squishy!" Miles cried. "Mom bought some at the store yesterday."

Nonni Lidia laughed. "They don't start out that way," she said. "The birds are actually quite *EGGS-traordinary*."

"Oh, Nonni," Olivia groaned.

"Can you tell us a story about chickens?" Julia asked. "With *no* scary foxes."

"I know lots of chicken stories," said Nonni Lidia. "As a girl, I helped raise them on my grandparents' farm. And, yes, sometimes there *were* foxes, but our faithful dog, Bobbi, did a good job of chasing them away.

"Our chickens were a lively bunch, wandering freely, munching on insects, worms, and grasses as they pleased. I loved watching a chicken chase down a grasshopper. And the lone rooster would strut this way and that, marking his territory and guarding the flock. King of the coop!

"I helped Nonna Rosa collect eggs twice a day. The chickens laid eggs neatly in their nest boxes—unlike the troublesome geese that laid wherever they pleased. Grandmother knew each chicken's squawk and which to check for a fresh egg.

"We didn't have much then, and an egg was a perfect meal by itself—delicious and full of healthy protein and vitamins.

"And the things Nonna Rosa could do with a fresh chicken, using every part to make scrumptious soups, sauces, and stews!

"In the spring, Nonna Rosa would set aside twenty eggs for hatching, allowing hens to *brood*, or sit on, the eggs and keep them warm. For twenty days or more, the brooding hens would sit and sit, barely stopping to eat or drink. Such steadfast mothers!

"I was fascinated by the magic happening inside those little shells. And, oh, the joy when those first little wobbly chicks poked out, with a loud chirp and their soft feathers still slick and wet.

"Now," Nonni Lidia said to the children. "Time to get some sleep before the roosters start crowing."

She tucked them all in and turned off the light.

Julia quickly fell asleep, dreaming of happy chicken families and *not* sneaky foxes.

The next morning Miles and Nonni Lidia were the first ones up.

"How would you like to help me make a great big frittata for breakfast?" she asked. "It's a bit like an omelet."

They gathered the ingredients and quickly got to work. Miles washed the scallions and asparagus, and Nonni Lidia chopped them into neat little piles.

Then Miles whisked the eggs and cream in a bowl, and Nonni Lidia tossed in salt, pepper, and leftover bread cut in small cubes.

"Now for my secret ingredient," Nonni Lidia said, winking at Miles. "Fresh ricotta."

"*Ri-cot-TA frit-ta-TA*," Miles sang. "That's fun to say."

At breakfast the children gobbled up delicious frittata and fresh fruit.

"Looks like I'll need more eggs," Nonni Lidia said.

"We could go to the store," suggested Olivia.

"Even better," said Nonni Lidia. "Let's go straight to the farm."

"A farm? Cool!" Ethan said. "I wonder if they'll have brown cows? They make chocolate milk."

Nonni Lidia shook her head and laughed.

In the car, everyone was excited for the trip to the farm. Olivia taught the other children the Chicken Dance.

"Like this," she said, showing them the funny moves she had learned at a wedding. On the backseat everyone wiggled their bottoms and flapped their chicken wings wildly.

"This is one crazy coop!" Nonni Lidia said.

Houses grew farther and farther apart. There were more trees and lots of wide-open, green land.

"We're here," Nonni Lidia said, making one final turn.

Farmer Hobbs greeted the children. "Welcome to my farm," he said. "Who wants to see some chickens?"

"We do!" the children shouted.

Farmer Hobbs led them out to a pasture dotted neatly with chicken coops. Chickens large and small wandered this way and that. There were black-and-white speckled chickens, chickens with reddish feathers, and white fluffy chickens that looked like they were wearing fuzzy hats.

A rooster swaggered by, his crimson cock's comb bouncing jauntily.

"Look at that funny thing on his head," Julia cried.

"That's Big Ben," said Farmer Hobbs. "Ol' Ben thinks he's pretty important, but the truth is, hens can lay eggs even without a rooster. He *is* a good alarm clock, though, and he does make quite a ruckus if the flock's in danger."

"Nonni, these chickens can walk all around just like the ones in Nonna Rosa's courtyard," said Lorenzo.

"We call it '*free-range*,'" said Farmer Hobbs. "We give them some feed too, in case they don't find enough to eat on their own."

He let Lorenzo and Julia scoop some food into the feeders.

At the coops, the children collected eggs, gently removing them from nest boxes. "This is more fun than an Easter Egg hunt," said Ethan.

There were big eggs and small eggs. Eggs in shades of brown, white, and cream, also pale greens and blues. Some were even reddish and pink.

"In the grocery store, most people only see white or brown eggs that are all about the same size," said Farmer Hobbs. "But different breeds of chickens lay eggs in all different sizes and colors."

The children happily helped Farmer Hobbs gather eggs and tend to the chickens, as the yolk-yellow sun sank lower in the sky. Nonni Lidia checked her watch.

"We better get going," she told the children. "Your parents will be coming to collect *you* soon, and we still need to cook."

The children thanked Farmer Hobbs for sharing his farm with them.

"Please take this for your supper," Farmer Hobbs said, giving Nonni Lidia a big bag packed with fresh chicken parts. "I kept in all the good bits like the feet and the neck." Nonni Lidia thanked Farmer Hobbs and shuttled the gang back to the car.

"Eggs!" Nonni Lidia cried, when they were almost home. "We forgot the eggs!"

Luckily, a supermarket was nearby. Nonni Lidia and the children rushed inside and headed for the cold section.

There were lots of choices.

"*Organic*," said Olivia.

"*Free-range*," said Miles.

"Look!" said Ethan. "They have Farmer Hobbs's eggs."

Back in Nonni Lidia's kitchen, the cooking quickly got underway.

Nonni Lidia showed the children a simple way to make fresh pasta. Ethan and Julia mixed together eggs, olive oil, and water, and then added the mixture to a bowl of flour Lorenzo had measured. They took turns squishing the dough together until it was a nice, smooth ball.

"We'll let that rest for a bit, then roll it out and cut it into strips," Nonni Lidia said. "Easy peasy."

As the children's parents began to arrive, fresh chicken sauce simmered away on the stove, filling the air with delicious smells.

This evening was mild and perfect for eating outside.

"Voilà!" said Olivia, as she presented a huge platter of fresh pasta topped with a delicious sauce of soft, shredded chicken meat.

"*Mmm, mmm.* This looks chicken-*licious*," Nonni Mima said.

The children buzzed with stories of the sleepover and the farm. Ethan tried eating with just his beak, and Olivia challenged everyone to a chicken dance-off after dinner.

Nonni Lidia looked around the table smiled at her lively brood. They were truly *egg-stra* special, and she was prouder than a mother hen.

Recipes...

FRIED POTATOES AND EGGS

Patate Fritte con Uova

This recipe serves two, but it can be easily doubled or cut in half. Potatoes and eggs cooked like this are best when prepared from start to end in the same pan, so the potatoes stay crispy and hot. You might want to do one panful at a time the first time you try this recipe, but once you eat this, I guarantee it will become a favorite and soon you'll get the knack of working two pans at once. Serve for breakfast or as lunch with a salad.

Yield: Serves 2

1 large Idaho potato
  (about 8 ounces)

⅓ cup extra-virgin olive oil

½ teaspoon fresh rosemary leaves

4 large eggs

Salt (preferably sea salt)

Freshly ground pepper

1. Peel the potato and cut it in half crosswise. Stand the halves cut side down and cut into ¼-inch slices, then cut the slices into ¼-inch strips. Pour the oil in a large nonstick skillet over medium-high heat. Add the potatoes and cook, shaking the pan and turning the potatoes as necessary, until they are golden on all sides, about 6 minutes. Hold the potatoes in place with a slotted spoon or wire skimmer while you pour off all but about 1 to 2 teaspoons of oil from the skillet. Return the skillet to the heat, add the rosemary leaves and toss well. Break the eggs into the pan.

2. Season generously with salt and pepper, and mix the potatoes and eggs together with a fork until the egg is cooked to your liking. Serve hot.

KIDS CAN:

Break and whisk eggs and pluck rosemary leaves.

RICOTTA FRITTATA

Frittata con Ricotta

Yield: Serves 4 to 6

3 tablespoons extra-virgin olive oil

1 large onion, sliced ¼ inch thick

1 ripe large tomato,
 sliced ½ inch thick

½ teaspoon kosher salt

8 large eggs

8 large basil leaves, shredded

½ cup Grana Padano, grated

6 tablespoons fresh ricotta,
 drained

1. Preheat the oven to 375°F. Heat oil in a 10-inch nonstick skillet over medium heat. Add onions and cook until softened, about 5 to 6 minutes. Drain and dry the tomato slices on paper towels; season with salt. Push the onion slices to one side of the skillet, and lay the tomato slices in one layer in the cleared space. Sear the tomato, turning once until the slices soften just at the edges, about 30 seconds per side. Remove the tomatoes to a plate and let the onions continue to cook while you prepare the eggs.

2. In a bowl, beat the eggs with the salt. Stir in basil and ¼ cup of the grated cheese until well mixed. Spread the onion slices in an even layer in the bottom of the skillet and pour the eggs on top. Reduce heat to medium-low and let cook until the eggs begin to set around the edges of the pan, about 2 to 3 minutes.

3. Arrange tomato slices on top of the frittata and drop tablespoons of the ricotta between the tomato slices. Sprinkle all over with the remaining grated cheese. Bake frittata until set all the way through and the top is golden, about 18 minutes. Let rest for a few minutes, then run a knife around the edge of the skillet and invert onto a plate or cutting board. Serve in wedges, warm or at room temperature.

KIDS CAN:

Shred basil—younger kids can roll up the leaves and snip with scissors
and break and whisk the eggs with the salt.

Oregano and Eggs

Uova all'Oregano

Yield: Serves 4

2 tablespoons extra-virgin olive oil

8 large eggs (2 each)

¼ teaspoon kosher salt

½ teaspoon dried oregano, preferably Sicilian oregano on the branch

¼ cup Grana Padano or Parmigiano-Reggiano, grated

1. Set a large (12-inch) nonstick skillet over a burner that is still off. Swirl the pan with the oil and gently break all the eggs to fill the pan, taking care not to break the yolks. An easy way is to break the eggs into a cup and then slide them out into the frying pan. Sprinkle with the salt and dried oregano. Sprinkle the grated cheese over all.

2. Cover the skillet and turn the flame to medium-low. Cook until the whites are set and the yolks are done to your liking, about 7 to 8 minutes for still-runny yolks.

KIDS CAN:

Break the eggs into cups (letting the adult slide them into the skillet) and crumble the oregano from the branch.

Sausage, Egg, and Peppers Sandwich

Panino con Frittata di Peperoni e Salsiccia

Yield: Makes 2 (6-inch) subs or 4 rolls

2 tablespoons extra-virgin olive oil

2 links sweet Italian sausage,
   removed from casing
   (about 8 ounces)

1 medium onion, thinly sliced

1 large red bell pepper,
   sliced ½ inch thick

¾ teaspoon kosher salt, divided

4 large eggs

2 (6-inch) lengths Italian bread,
   split and toasted or 4 crusty
   rolls, split and toasted

1. In a large nonstick skillet over medium heat, heat oil. When the oil is hot, add the sausage. Cook, crumbling the sausage with a wooden spoon, until the sausage is no longer pink, about 3 minutes. Add the onion and bell pepper. Season with ½ teaspoon salt, cover, and cook until wilted and lightly caramelized, about 10 minutes.

2. Beat the eggs in a bowl with the remaining ¼ teaspoon salt. When the peppers and onions are wilted, pour the eggs into the skillet and cook until just set, but still a little wet, about 1 to 2 minutes. Remove from heat; the eggs will finish cooking off the heat.

3. Pile the eggs on bread or rolls and serve immediately.

KIDS CAN:

Break and whisk the eggs, and older kids can slice the vegetables.

BAKED STUFFED SHELLS

Conchiglie Ripiene al Forno

Apound of "jumbo" pasta shells contains about thirty-six. This recipe makes enough filling for about thirty shells, so it's likely you'll have a few extras, which may come in handy as some shells break in the box or during cooking. Be sure to cook the shells very al dente before filling them, or they will tear when you try to stuff them.

Individual servings of stuffed shells make an impressive presentation. If you have enough individual baking dishes, divide the shells and sauce among them, then top with cheese, keeping in mind that you might need a little more cheese to top individual servings than is called for in the recipe.

Yield: Serves 6
(about 5 stuffed shells for each person)

1½ pounds fresh ricotta or packaged whole milk ricotta

1 (35-ounce) can peeled Italian plum tomatoes (preferably San Marzano)

Salt

1 pound fresh mozzarella cheese

1 cup Parmigiano-Reggiano cheese, freshly grated

⅓ cup fresh Italian parsley, chopped

Freshly ground white pepper

1 large egg

¼ cup extra-virgin olive oil

6 garlic cloves, crushed

¼ teaspoon crushed red pepper

10 fresh basil leaves

1 pound jumbo pasta shells

1. Place the ricotta in a cheesecloth-lined sieve and set the sieve over a bowl. Cover the ricotta with plastic wrap and place in the refrigerator for at least 8 hours up to one day. Discard the liquid from the bowl.

2. Pass the tomatoes through a food mill fitted with the fine disc. (If you do not have a food mill, seed the tomatoes and place them in a food processor. Process the tomatoes, using quick on/off pulses, until they are finely ground. Don't overprocess or you will incorporate air into the tomatoes and change their texture and color.) Meanwhile, bring 6 quarts of salted water to a boil in an 8-quart pot over high heat.

3. Slice half the mozzarella thin and cut the remaining half into ¼-inch cubes. Turn the drained ricotta into a mixing bowl. Mix in the mozzarella cubes, grated cheese, and parsley. Season to taste with salt and white pepper. Beat the egg well and stir it into the ricotta mixture.

4. Heat the oil in a large skillet over medium heat. Scatter the garlic over the oil and cook until golden brown, shaking the pan, about 2 minutes. Lower the tomatoes close to the skillet and carefully pour them into the skillet. Add the crushed red pepper and season lightly with salt. Bring the sauce to a quick boil, then adjust the heat until the sauce is simmering. Cook until the sauce is lightly thickened, about 30 minutes. Stir the basil into the sauce a few minutes before it is done.

5. Meanwhile, stir the shells into the boiling water. Return to a boil, stirring frequently. Cook the pasta, semicovered, stirring occasionally, until softened, but still quite firm, about 7 minutes. Fish the shells out of the water with a large skimmer and carefully lower them into a bowl of cold water. Drain them carefully.

6. Preheat the oven to 425°F. Line the bottom of a 9 x 13-inch baking dish with about ³/₄ cup of the tomato sauce. Spoon about 2 tablespoons of the ricotta mixture into each shell. The shell should be filled to capacity but not overstuffed. Nestle the shells next to each other in the baking dish as you fill them. Spoon the remaining sauce over the shells, coating each one. Arrange the slices of mozzarella in an even layer over the shells. Bake until the mozzarella is browned and bubbling, about 25 minutes. Remove and let stand 5 minutes before serving.

KIDS CAN:

Mix ricotta mixture; help stuff the shells with a teaspoon;
and crank the tomatoes through the food mill. (It's messy, so wear an apron!)

ROMAN "EGG DROP" SOUP

Stracciatella alla Romana

Stracciare means "to rip to shreds" in Italian, and, indeed, that is how this soup looks after stirring some beaten eggs with some grated cheese in a good chicken broth. Once you have a good chicken broth, the rest is easy. Stracciatella is usually served with shredded spinach and beaten egg, but I recall having it with just egg and cheese when spinach was not in season. In the Italy that I grew up in, seasons made a difference, not only in how we dressed, but in what we ate. This a great restorative soup, used in most Italian families.

Yield: Serves 6

8 cups defatted homemade chicken stock

1¼ teaspoons kosher salt, divided

4 cups packed spinach leaves, shredded (or baby spinach leaves)

4 large eggs

⅓ cup Grana Padano or Parmigiano-Reggiano, grated, plus more for serving

Freshly ground black pepper

1. In a medium pot, bring the stock to a simmer with 1 teaspoon salt. Once the stock is simmering, add spinach and cook until tender, about 3 minutes.

2. Meanwhile, in a medium bowl, whisk together the eggs, grated cheese, the remaining ¼ teaspoon salt, and some freshly ground black pepper to taste.

3. Once the spinach is tender, add about ⅓ of the egg mixture to the soup, while continuously whisking, to make shreds of eggs. Add the remaining eggs in 2 more batches, letting the soup return to a boil between additions. Once all of the eggs have been added, bring soup to a final boil and use the whisk to break up any large clusters of eggs. Serve soup with additional grated cheese.

KIDS CAN:

Wash and shred spinach (baby spinach doesn't need to be shredded, just washed) and break and whisk eggs with the grated cheese.

LIDIA'S CAPPELLINI WITH SPAGHETTI SQUASH (OR ZUCCHINI), CHICKEN, AND GRANA PADANO

Cappellini con zucca, pollo e Grana Padano

1 small spaghetti squash or
   1 medium zucchini

1 teaspoon coarse sea salt or
   kosher salt or to taste plus
   more for cooking pasta

⅓ cup extra-virgin olive oil

4 plump garlic cloves, crushed

1 small onion, thinly sliced
   (1 cup of slices)

½ pound ground chicken or
   turkey breast

1 (28-ounce) can Italian plum
   tomatoes, preferably San
   Marzano, (crushed by hand)
   or one jar of Lidia's Tomato
   Basil Sauce

1 pound Lidia's Capellini

8 shredded basil leaves

1 cup Grana Padano,
   freshly grated

KIDS CAN:

Crush canned tomatoes by hand
in a big bowl; shred cooked,
cooled spaghetti squash with a
fork or shred zucchini on the
grater (hold the zucchini in a
kitchen towel to avoid getting
scraped on the box grater); shred
basil, by hand or with scissors;
and crush garlic (if too young for a
knife, it can be crushed with the
bottom of a can).

Yield: Serves 6

1. Split the spaghetti squash in half, season with salt, and bake in a preheated 400°F oven for 20 minutes. Then let cool and with the tines of a fork scrape the spaghetti-like strands from the inside of the squash. Loosen the strands. Or wash and shred the zucchini on the coarse holes of a box grater. You will need 2 cups of either spaghetti squash or shredded zucchini.

2. Pour the oil into the big skillet and set over medium-high heat. Scatter in the sliced garlic and let it start sizzling. Stir in the onion slices and cook for a couple of minutes to wilt. Stir in the ground chicken or turkey, and cook for 5 minutes. Add in all the spaghetti squash, or shredded zucchini, and season with salt. With tongs, toss all together and cook for 5 minutes.

3. Pour in the crushed tomatoes along with a ½ cup of water sloshed in the tomato containers, or the one jar of Lidia's Tomato Basil Sauce. Stir well and cover; when the tomato juices are boiling, adjust the heat to keep them bubbling gently. Cook covered for about 10 minutes (if using canned tomatoes, cook for 15 minutes), stirring occasionally. When the vegetables are softened, uncover and continue cooking to reduce the pan juices to a good consistency for dressing the pasta, about 5 minutes. Adjust the seasoning to taste and keep at a low simmer.

4. While the sauce is cooking, heat the salted pasta cooking water to a rolling boil (at least 6 quarts water and a tablespoon salt). Drop in the capellini and cook until barely al dente. Lift them from the water, drain them for a moment, and then drop them into the simmering sauce. Toss and cook all together for a couple of minutes, over moderate heat. Moisten the pasta with pasta water if it seems dry (about ½ cup) or cook rapidly to reduce the juices in the skillet if it is too saucy.

5. When the pasta is perfectly cooked and enveloped by the sauce, turn off the heat. Throw in the shredded basil leaves and the grated cheese and toss all together well with the pasta. Serve nice and hot.

Spaghetti with Egg, Onion, and Bacon

Spaghetti alla Carbonara

Yield: Serves 6

Kosher salt

1 pound spaghetti

6 ounces bacon, chopped

Extra-virgin olive oil, if needed

1 small onion, chopped
(about 1 cup)

2 large egg yolks

⅓ cup parsley, chopped

1 teaspoon freshly ground
black pepper

1 cup Grana Padano or
Parmigiano-Reggiano, grated

1. Bring a large pot of salted water to boil. When the sauce made in the steps below is about halfway cooked (about 6 to 7 minutes), drop the spaghetti into the boiling pasta water and stir.

2. Cook the bacon in a skillet over medium heat until the fat has mostly rendered, about 4 to 5 minutes. (If your bacon is very lean, you can add a drizzle of oil to help start the rendering of the fat.) Push the bacon to one side of the pan, and add the onion. Let both cook separately until the onion is tender, about 8 minutes, then mix the two back together. (If you like, you can drain off the excess bacon fat here and replace it with oil.) Ladle 2 cups pasta water into the skillet with the bacon and onion, bring to a rapid boil, and quickly reduce the sauce.

3. Meanwhile, whisk the egg yolks with ¼ cup hot pasta water in a small bowl. When the sauce has reduced by about half and the spaghetti is al dente, scoop the pasta into the sauce with tongs or a spider. Add the chopped parsley, pepper, and salt to taste. Toss the pasta until it is coated in the sauce.

4. Remove the pan from the fire, and quickly mix in the egg yolks and water mixture, stirring until creamy. Toss the pasta with the grated cheese, and serve immediately.

KIDS CAN:

Whisk eggs with parsley, pepper, and salt; wash and chop parsley; and grate and toss the cheese.

TRADITIONAL RICE AND CHICKEN

Pollo e Riso alla Pitocca

Yield: Serves 4 to 6

1½ pounds boneless, skinless chicken thighs

1 cup onion, cut in 1-inch chunks

1 cup carrot, cut in 1-inch chunks

1 cup celery, cut in 1-inch chunks

2 plump garlic cloves, peeled

⅓ cup extra-virgin olive oil

2 teaspoons kosher salt, divided

1 fresh bay leaf

½ cup dry white wine (optional)

5 cups hot chicken or turkey stock, plus more if needed

2 cups Italian short-grain rice, such as Arborio, Carnaroli, or Vialone Nano for finishing

2 tablespoons butter, cut in pieces

3 tablespoons fresh Italian parsley, chopped

½ cup Grana Padano, grated, plus more for passing

1. Trim any excess fat from the chicken thighs, and cut them into 1-inch chunks. Using a food processor, mince the onion, carrot, celery, and garlic into a fine-textured paste or "pestata." Pour the oil in the saucepan, and set over medium-high heat. Stir in the pestata, and season with 1 teaspoon of the salt. Cook for about 5 minutes, stirring frequently, until the pestata has dried and begins to stick to the bottom of the pan. Toss in the chicken pieces and the bay leaf, and sprinkle the remaining teaspoon of salt over it. Tumble and stir the chicken in the pan until browned and caramelized all over, about 4 minutes.

2. Raise the heat, pour in the white wine, if using, and cook, stirring and scraping up the browned bits in the pan, until the wine has almost completely evaporated.

3. Pour in the hot stock, stirring, then all the rice. Bring to a boil over high heat, cover the pan, and reduce the heat to low to keep the rice bubbling gently. Cook for about 14 minutes, or until both the rice and the chicken chunks are fully cooked and the consistency is creamy.

4. Turn off the heat, drop in the butter pieces, and stir until thoroughly incorporated, then stir in the parsley and ½ cup of grated cheese. Spoon the riso into warm pasta bowls and serve immediately, adding additional grated cheese at the table.

KIDS CAN:

Help pulse the pestata in the food processor; crush and peel the garlic; peel the carrots; cut the butter into pieces; and pluck (and chop, if older) the parsley leaves.

CHICKEN PARMIGIANA

Pollo alla Parmigiana

Yield: Serves 6

6 (6- to 8-ounce) boneless
skinless chicken breasts

½ teaspoon kosher salt

Freshly ground black pepper

All-purpose flour, for dredging

2 cups dry breadcrumbs

2 large eggs

Vegetable oil, for frying

8 large basil leaves, shredded

3 cups marinara

8 ounces low-moisture
mozzarella, shredded

½ cup Grana Padano or
Parmigiano-Reggiano, grated

1. Preheat the oven to 425°F.

2. Lightly pound the chicken breasts, just to make them an even thickness. Season the chicken with the salt and pepper.

3. Spread flour and breadcrumbs on 2 rimmed plates. Beat the eggs in a wide shallow bowl. Dredge the chicken in flour, tapping off the excess. Dip the chicken in egg, letting the excess drip back into the bowl. Coat the chicken on all sides in the breadcrumbs.

4. Heat ½ inch vegetable oil in a large skillet over medium heat. When the oil is hot, add the chicken, in batches if necessary. Cook until browned and crispy, about 4 minutes per side. Drain on paper towels.

5. Stir shredded basil into the marinara. In a medium bowl, toss together the grated cheeses.

6. In a baking dish large enough to fit the chicken in one layer, spread 1½ cups of the marinara. Lay the chicken breasts on the sauce. Top with remaining marinara. Sprinkle with the grated cheeses. Bake until chicken is cooked through and topping is browned and bubbly, about 20 to 25 minutes.

KIDS CAN:

Pound chicken breasts; whisk the eggs; help with the breading (though it's messy, it's also fun); toss the grated cheeses together; and help layer the chicken, sauce, and cheese in the baking dish.

Breast of Chicken in a Light Lemon-Herb Sauce

Involtini di Pollo al Salmoriglio

6 boneless, skinless chicken breasts (about 5 ounces each)

½ cup fine dry breadcrumbs

¼ cup extra-virgin olive oil, divided

3 tablespoons fresh Italian parsley, chopped, divided

1½ teaspoons dried oregano, preferably the Sicilian or Greek type dried on the branch, crumbled, divided

Salt

1 cup dry white wine

½ cup chicken stock or canned, reduced-sodium chicken broth

¼ cup fresh lemon juice

Pinch of crushed red pepper (optional)

4 garlic cloves, peeled

Yield: Serves 4

1. Preheat the oven to 450°F. Cut each chicken breast in half crosswise on a diagonal to yield two pieces of roughly equal size. Place two pieces at a time between two sheets of plastic wrap. Pound gently with the flat side of a meat mallet or the bottom of a small heavy saucepan to flatten them slightly to about ½ inch thick.

2. Toss the breadcrumbs, 1 tablespoon of the oil, 1 tablespoon of the chopped parsley, ½ teaspoon of the oregano, and salt to taste, together in a bowl until blended. Spread 1 teaspoon of the breadcrumb mixture over each piece of chicken, reserving the remaining crumbs. Roll each chicken piece into a compact shape and fasten securely with a toothpick.

3. Arrange the filled chicken breasts side by side in a 9 x13-inch, preferably flameproof baking dish. (There should be some space between each piece of chicken.) Stir the wine, stock, lemon juice, red pepper (if using), the remaining 3 tablespoons oil, the remaining teaspoon of oregano, and salt to taste, together in a small bowl. Pour into the baking dish. Whack the garlic with the flat side of a knife and scatter them among the chicken pieces. Bake 10 minutes.

4. Top the chicken with the remaining breadcrumb mixture. Return to the oven and bake until the breadcrumb topping is golden brown, about 8 to 10 minutes more.

5. If the roasting pan is flameproof, place it directly over medium-high heat, add the remaining 2 tablespoons parsley, and bring the pan juices to a boil. Boil until lightly thickened, 1 to 2 minutes. (If the roasting pan is not flameproof, transfer the chicken rolls to a warm platter and pour the juices into a skillet before bringing them to a boil.) Remove the garlic cloves, or leave them in if you like. Gently transfer the chicken pieces to plates with a slotted spoon. Pull the toothpicks from the chicken without loosening the breadcrumb topping. Pour the sauce around, not over, the chicken pieces and serve immediately.

KIDS CAN:

Toss together the breadcrumb mixture; help pound the chicken; juice the lemons; pluck the parsley leaves and chop (if older); and crush and peel the garlic.

My Mother's Chicken and Potatoes
(with My Special Touches)

Pollo e patate alla Nonna Erminia

In my family, favorite dishes are always being altered according to what is available and what is best—especially when I'm cooking.

Here's a perfect example: chicken and potatoes, fried together in a big skillet so they are crisp and moist at the same time, is my mother's specialty. Growing up, my brother and I demanded it every week; our kids, Tanya and Joe and Eric, Paul and Estelle, clamored for it too. And now the next generation of little ones are asking their great-grandmother to make chicken and potatoes for them.

Yield: Serves 4

Basic Chicken and Potatoes

2½ pounds chicken legs or assorted pieces (bone in)

½ cup canola oil

½ teaspoon salt or more to taste, divided

1 pound red bliss potatoes, preferably no bigger than 2 inches across

2 tablespoons extra-virgin olive oil or more

2 medium onions, peeled and quartered lengthwise

2 short branches of fresh rosemary with plenty of needles

My Special Touches— Try Either or Both

4 to 6 ounces sliced bacon (5 or 6 slices)

1 or 2 pickled cherry peppers, sweet or hot, or none, or more!—cut in half and seeded (optional)

1. Rinse the chicken pieces and pat dry with paper towels. Trim off excess skin and all visible fat. Cut the drumsticks from the thighs. If using breast halves, cut into 2 small pieces.

2. Make the bacon roll-ups: cut the bacon slices in half crosswise and roll each strip into a neat, tight cylinder. Stick a toothpick through the roll to secure it; cut or break the toothpick so only a tiny bit sticks out (allowing the bacon to roll around and cook evenly).

3. Pour the canola oil into the skillet and set over high heat. Sprinkle the chicken with ¼ teaspoon salt on all sides. When the oil is very hot, lay the pieces skin side down, an inch or so apart—watch out for oil spatters. Don't crowd the chicken: if necessary fry it in batches, similar pieces (like drumsticks) together.

4. Drop the bacon roll-ups into the oil around the chicken, turning and shifting them often. Let the chicken fry in place for several minutes to brown on the underside, then turn and continue frying until they are golden brown on all sides, 7 to 10 minutes or more. Fry breast pieces, only for 5 or so minutes, taking them out of the oil with tongs as soon as they are golden. Let the bacon roll-ups cook and get lightly crisp, but not dark, taking them out as they are done cooking. Adjust the heat to maintain steady sizzling and coloring.

Meanwhile, rinse and dry the potatoes. Slice each one through the middle on the axis that gives the largest cut surface, then toss them with the olive oil and ¼ teaspoon salt.

6. When all the chicken and bacon is cooked and out of the skillet, pour off the frying oil. Return the skillet to medium heat and put in all the potatoes cut side down in a single layer into the hot pan. With a spatula, scrape all the oil out of the mixing bowl into the skillet; drizzle over a bit more oil if the pan seems dry. Fry and crisp the potatoes for about 4 minutes to form a crust, then move them around the pan, still cut side down, until they are all brown and crisp, 7 minutes or more. Turn them over and fry another 2 minutes to cook and crisp on their rounded skin sides.

7. Still over medium heat, add the onion wedges and rosemary branches to the pan with the potatoes and toss the ingredients around the pan. If using cherry peppers (either hot or sweet), cut the seeded halves into ½-inch wide pieces and scatter them in the pan too.

8. Return the chicken pieces—except breast pieces—to the pan, along with the bacon roll-ups; pour in any chicken juices that have accumulated. Raise the heat slightly, and carefully turn and tumble the chicken, potatoes, and onion (and bacon and/or pepper pieces), so they are heating and getting coated with pan juices—but take care not to break the potato pieces. Spread everything out in the pan—potatoes on the bottom as much as possible to keep crisping up—and cover.

9. Lower the heat to medium and cook for about 7 minutes, shaking the pan occasionally, then uncover and toss all the ingredients again. Cover and cook another 7 minutes or so, adding the breast pieces at this point. Give everything another toss. Cook covered for 10 minutes more.

10. Remove the cover, turn the pieces again, and cook in the open skillet for about 10 minutes to evaporate the moisture and caramelize everything. Taste a bit of potato (or chicken) for salt and sprinkle on more as needed. Turn the pieces now and then. When they are all glistening and golden, and the potatoes are cooked through, remove the skillet from the stove, and bring it right to the table. Serve portions of chicken and potatoes, or let people help themselves.

KIDS CAN:

Halve the potatoes and make the bacon roll-ups.

ZABAGLIONE WITH BERRIES

Zabaglione con frutti di bosco

Yield: About 2 cups

6 large egg yolks,
  at room temperature

¼ cup dry Marsala wine

¼ cup granulated sugar

Fresh fruit or berries, for serving

1. In a medium-size copper or other heatproof bowl, whisk the egg yolks, Marsala wine, and sugar together until smooth. Place over, not in, barely simmering water and continue beating (switching to a hand-held electric mixer at medium speed, if you like) until the mixture is pale yellow and frothy and falls back on itself in thick ribbons when the whisk or beaters are lifted, about 6 to 8 minutes. If the mixture is not beat consistently, the egg yolks will cook and the mixture will appear curdled.

2. Remove the sauce from the heat and serve immediately, spooned either into individual cups or over fresh fruit or berries.

KIDS CAN:

Help separate the eggs (Lidia's trick: Break the egg into the palm of your hand and let the white slip through into a bowl; put the yolk in another bowl); whisk the yolks, sugar, and marsala together before it goes on the heat; and help prep the berries.

RICOTTA COOKIES

Biscotti di Ricotta

Yield: Makes about 3½ dozen

2¼ cups all-purpose flour

1 teaspoon baking powder

Pinch kosher salt

1 cup granulated sugar

½ cup (1 stick) unsalted butter,
  at room temperature

2 large eggs

8 ounces fresh ricotta, drained

½ teaspoon vanilla extract

Zest of ½ lemon

Glaze

2 cups confectioners' sugar, sifted

Zest of other ½ lemon,
  plus ¼ cup lemon juice

1. Preheat the oven to 325°F. Sift together flour, baking powder, and salt into a bowl, and set aside.

2. Line two baking sheets with parchment paper.

3. Cream the sugar and butter in a mixer fitted with the paddle attachment on high speed until light and fluffy, about 2 minutes. Reduce the speed to medium, and crack in the eggs one at a time, beating well between additions. Add the ricotta, vanilla, and lemon zest, and beat to combine. Add the flour mixture, and beat on low until just combined, but do not overmix.

4. Drop the dough in heaping rounded tablespoons onto the baking sheets. Place in the oven, and bake, rotating pans halfway through the baking time (about 9 to 10 minutes), until the cookies are puffed, golden, and cooked all the way through, about 18 to 20 minutes total. Remove from the oven, and cool on wire racks.

5. When the cookies are completely cool, make the glaze. In a bowl, whisk together the confectioners' sugar, lemon juice, and zest to make a smooth glaze. Adjust the consistency with a little water or more confectioners' sugar to make the glaze thick enough to stick to the cookies when dipped. Hold each cookie with two fingers, then dip the top of the cookies in the glaze and let dry on the racks until all are done. Let dry for 2 hours before storing.

KIDS CAN:

Sift dry ingredients; add the ingredients into the mixer; help drop cookies onto baking sheet with a teaspoon
or soup spoon; and help dip cookies in the glaze.